A Small Song
Published in Great Britain in 2016 by Graffeg Limited

Text and photographs by Karin Celestine
copyright © 2016.
Designed and produced by Graffeg Limited
copyright © 2016

Graffeg Limited, 24 Stradey Park Business
Centre, Mwrwg Road, Llangennech, Llanelli,
Carmarthenshire SA14 8YP Wales UK
Tel 01554 824000 www.graffeg.com

Karin Celestine is hereby identified as the author
of this work in accordance with section 77 of the
Copyrights, Designs and Patents Act 1988.

A CIP Catalogue record for this book is available
from the British Library.

ISBN 9781910862414

1 2 3 4 5 6 7 8 9

For more fun with the Tribe visit
www.celestineandthehare.com

Celestine and the Hare
A Small Song
by Karin Celestine

This book belongs to

GRAFFEG

Meet the Tribe

Baby Weasus was found on the doorstep on Christmas Eve and was adopted by King Norty. She is only little but clever and brave and curious with a huge kind heart. Being a weasel she is also a little bit mischievous, especially when with her daddy.

King Norty is the King of the Weasels. He can't read but uses his weaselly intelligence, wit and torrential charm for choklit snaffling. Which is what he spends his days plotting to do (along with being daddy to Baby Weasus).

Panda loves the sea and his sock hat. He likes to draw and is best friends with Emily. He is quiet and thoughtful and loves it when Emily reads to him.

Emily is wise and patient and kind and loves to read. She looks after everyone in the Shed and gives the best cuddles. She likes to make things and read books but will always stop what she is doing to hold down the knot on your parcel.

Small doesn't remember what he is or where he came from before he was found but he is small so he is called Small. He is rather quiet and shy and sometimes people don't notice him, but he is very helpful and always kind. He likes to sit in tea cups and eat biscuits and watch what is going on best of all. Everyone loves Small.

Celestine and the Hare

Karin Celestine lives in a small house in Monmouth, Wales. In her garden there is a shed and in that shed is another world. The world of Celestine and the Hare.

It is a world where weasels are ruled by King Norty, pandas ride space hoppers and bears read stories to each other. It is a place that makes people smile and where kindness is the order of the day. All are welcome.

Karin taught children, about art, about chemistry, numbers, crafts and magic, but she was always drawn back to the Shed where she brings to life creatures of all kinds using only wool, observation and the power of imagination.

Karin and the creatures love stories and kindness, books and choklit and making things, and on Sundays they have Danish pastries but not the apricot ones because they are frankly wrong.

Celestine, her great grandmother and namesake, watches over all in the shed and the hare sits with her; old wisdom helping the Tribe along their path in life.

Celestine and the Hare
A Small Song

For my gentle dreamer Max
who has the music inside him.

Small and Baby Weasus love to play in the woods. One day they heard a sound. Baby Weasus had never heard anything like it before and it made her smile.

There, under a tree, was a hedgehog. Playing the banjo.

Small let out a little gasp and ran towards the music. He seemed to hold his breath. Listening.

The hedgehog played on and Small sat and listened and his heart seemed to fill with warmth and happiness and all he could hear was the music.

King Norty arrived to take them home.
'Daddy, Small won't come,' said Baby
Weasus pointing to the hedgehog.
'He said the music was inside him and now
he's just sat listening.'

'Let's just sit and wait here for him,'
said King Norty. 'You shouldn't hurry
someone lost in a memory.'

They sat and had a cuddle and waited for Small. Eventually the music stopped and Small, still very quiet, came over to them. King Norty held out a paw for him as they walked home.

At bedtime, Small spoke.

He said 'I remember.'

'What?' asked Baby Weasus.

'I remember something from where I come from. I remember my grandpa playing that song to me in my cot. I can't remember what he looked like but I can remember the song.'

When Small had fallen asleep, Baby
Weasus went to see her daddy.

'I wish he could hear that song again. It
made him so happy to hear it. I think it
was a little bit of home for him and he
doesn't remember anything of his home.'

'Hmm', said King Norty. 'You go to back
to bed now so Small is not alone
and I shall have a think...'

King Norty went out to the woods to see if he could find the hedgehog but when he got there, he had long gone. The badgers who were just waking up for the night said he was a travelling musician and wouldn't be back till next autumn.

King Norty walked back to the Shed
wondering what to do. He sat down to eat
some of his spare choklit hoard and the
box gave him an idea. He set to work.
Not many people know that he is an
excellent musician and in his younger days
he played the weasel horn in an orchestra.
He had a rummage around, found some
elastic bands and emptied the box.

He wound the rubber bands around the box. Every so often he would twang one of the bands, listen and then carry on.

He put a pencil in at one end and then he left the rubber band box he had made next to Small's bed and went back to counting his choklit hoard.

When Small awoke, he wasn't quite sure what was next to his bed. So he tried sitting on it and the rubber bands made a sound just like the banjo in the woods. 'Oh!' gasped Small and jumped up. He plucked at another rubber band and another and another, and a tune started to appear.

Every day Small practiced playing his banjo box and every day he managed to play a little bit better.

It took a long time and he kept making mistakes, but Small knows that you learn when you make mistakes so he kept practising and practising and practising...

After many months he was able to play the song his grandpa played to him quite well. Now, whenever he felt a bit unsure of who he was or where he came from, he could make music on his box banjo. 'Thank you, King Norty.'

You can make your own musical instruments

King Norty is going to show you how to make a banjo or guitar.

First you need a box. Something like a shoe box works well. King Norty used a postal box that he taped shut all the way round first.

Draw a circle on the top of the box, slightly to one side if it is a rectangle, or use the shape of the hole in a tissue box.

Cut the circle out. Take care
when poking a hole to get started
that you don't hurt yourself.

Once you have got your circle cut out, thread some rubber bands around the box. If you have different sizes, thread the thickest at one end, and the thinnest at the other. You can choose how many you want on there. You can have 4 like a violin or 6 like a guitar or banjo. Or even 12 if your box is big enough!

You need to make a bridge to stop the bands touching the box. You can use a piece of cardboard with notches cut in for each string or a pencil or piece of dowelling wood. When done, they should twang like a real instrument.

You can play around with the bands to get the sound you want.

If you press on the box, you can change the note played. Stretching the bands will make the note higher.

You can decorate it, or add a handle like a guitar if you want.

Use a wrapping paper tube, a ruler or a piece of cardboard. King Norty has drawn lines on his to make it look like a guitar.

If you want to play a real instrument, you can ask your family if they have one you can borrow or ask at school. Sometimes they have instruments you can borrow to learn and many schools do lessons too.

It can be fun to play in an orchestra or band with other people or you can play on your own. It takes a lot of practice to be able to play tunes but a few minutes every day and you'll soon be playing songs like the hedgehog.

Celestine and the Hare books

Celestine and the Hare
Small Finds a Home

Celestine and the Hare
Paper Boat for Panda

Celestine and the Hare
Honey for Tea

Celestine and the Hare
Finding your Place

Celestine and the Hare
A Small Song

Celestine and the Hare
Catching Dreams

Read about a small act of kindness in each of these six books and learn a new craft along the way. Send us pictures of your craft to the Tribe page on Graffeg's website.

Visit Graffeg website for details. www.graffeg.com